The Bongles and The Crafty Crows

Written by Oscar Van Heek   Illustrated by Dean Queazy

The Bongles

Meet Big Bubba!
He's really funny.
He wears his heart on his sleeve
and thinks with his tummy.

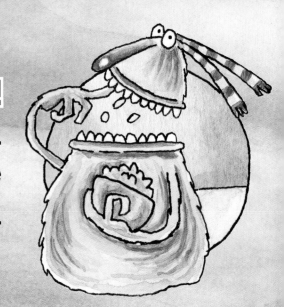

And this is Beanie,
keep up if you can.
She's full of ideas
when the team needs a plan.

The Twins share a tail
and look quite the same.
Double and Trouble,
by nature and name.

Meet Jessie.
She's the musical one.
Without her the Bongles
would have half as much fun.

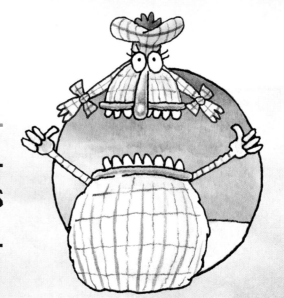

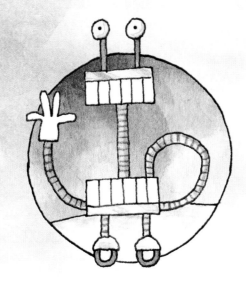

This is Pet Robot.
He's made from spare parts.
He can change into anything
and is dear to their hearts.

3

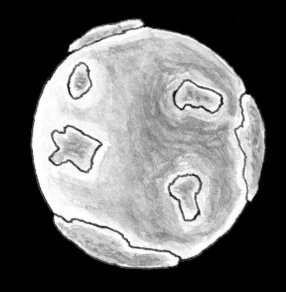

On a planet far far away,
the night was about
to make way for the day.

The Bongles were sleeping, dreaming away,
when three wooden crates drifted in to their bay.

One full of dishes
and one full of pies
and one full of clothes,
dresses and ties.

Jessie **was** pleased.
She loved her new clothes,
but she'd better beware,
because so did the crows.

They dived right in
got some pants and a shoe,
flapped their wings
and off they flew.

The Twins meanwhile,
stared into their crate,
then grabbed some glasses,
a cup and plate.

They started juggling
and threw them up to the sky,
but the crows swooped in
and they let out a cry.

10

Now Pet had been watching
and took matters in hand.
He called everyone over
and told them his plan.

They grabbed their crates
and away they sped,
and took their treasure
down to the shed.

Now all three crates
were safely inside.
It was time for a passcode,
which Bubba supplied.

He pondered
which numbers
would padlock the door.
He puzzled some more,
then chose
one, two, three, four.

15

Now feeling happy
that no one could breach
their lock on the door,
they left for the beach.

16

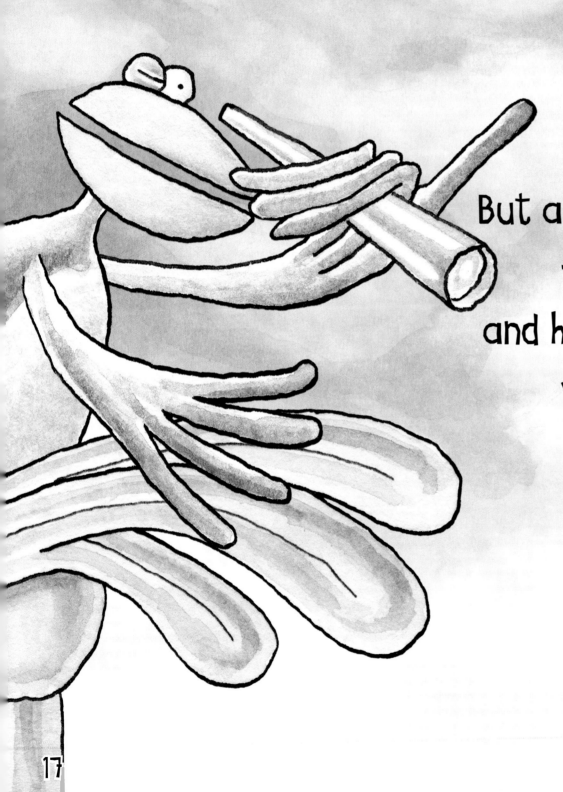

But a crow had been watching
from up in the trees,
and had spotted the passcode
with effortless ease.

He swooped right down,
set the numbers all in a row,
that opened the lock.
What a clever crow!

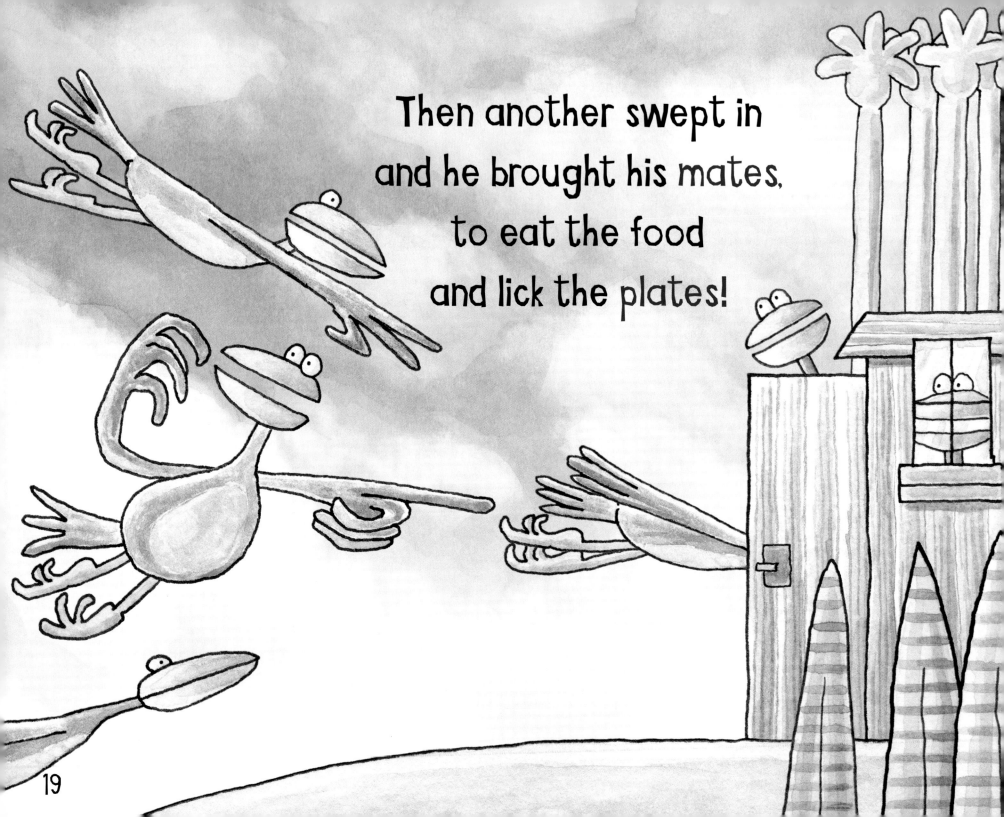

Then another swept in
and he brought his mates,
to eat the food
and lick the plates!

19

Squawking about,
and munching away,
they all dressed up
and began to play.

But Pet heard their noise,
and started to shout.
Waving his arms,
he soon drove them out!

Pet turned his tummy
into a screen
and asked for a password
to enter in the machine.

He then asked Jessie
to stand on her toes,
and hold out her coat
to shield them from the crows.

Bubba racked his brain,
chose three random words,
peas, trees...
and hummingbirds.

PEAS

TREES

HUMMINGBIRDS

24

Pet extended his arms,
and reached right round the hut,
then clasped his hands tight
and locked the door shut.

Now only Bubba
could unlock the door.
For his words were the key
to keep their treasure secure.

 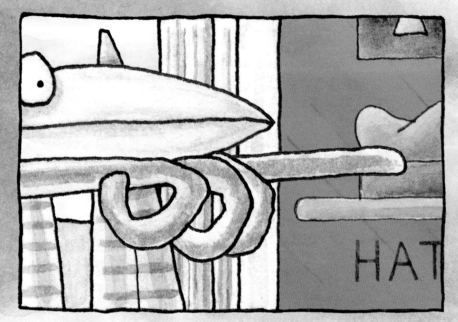

Soon the crows flew in
and entered three words,
but guessed the wrong ones.
Those silly birds!

CUP

Now after three goes
they got such a fright,
the alarm went off,
and they all took flight.

28

The Bongles cried
with tears of laughter.
Those silly crows.
What a disaster!

Pleased that their treasure
was safe and protected,
that not even the crows
could steal undetected.

Then Beanie filled glasses,
tapped them with a twig.
She struck out a rhythm
and they all did a jig.

One by one,
the crows came to see.
Witnessed the dancing
and watched on in glee.

Some wearing hats,
some wearing pants,
the crows were delighted
and did their own dance.

The Bongles fell about laughing.
Those crazy crows!
Now they were friends,
and no longer foes.

Ideas for Reading

Look at the cover and the character introductions.

1. What do you see on the front cover?

2. What does "crafty" mean?

3. Who are the characters, and do you have a favourite?

Read the book or watch the animation up to page 12.

1. What are the crows up to?

   "Now Pet had been watching and took matters in hand.
   He called everyone over, and told them his plan."

2. Why does Pet need a plan?

3. What was Pet's plan?

4. What would be your plan?

5. What things are special and important to you?

6. How do you keep your special and important things safe and secure?

Passcode or Password?

Passwords are similar to passcodes, but instead of numbers they use words.

Pet Robot used a password to keep the shed safe from the crows.

We use passwords to keep our information safe on digital devices and the internet.

You might have seen a grown-up using a passcode to unlock a mobile phone,

or a password to unlock a computer.

What makes a good passcode?

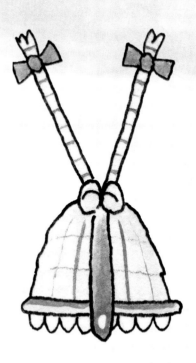

Read the book or watch the animation from pages 13 - 20.

1. What numbers did Bubba choose to make a passcode?

2. Was it secure?

3. What are random numbers?

4. Did Bubba choose random numbers?

5. What random numbers could Bubba have chosen instead?

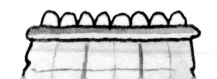

Read the book or watch the animation up to page 24.

"But a crow had been watching from up in the trees,
and had spotted the passcode with effortless ease."

1. How could the Bongles have avoided their passcode being unlocked by the crafty crows?
2. What did Jessie do to shield the password from the crows?

What makes a good password?

Read the book and or watch the animation up to page 34 .

"Bubba racked his brain, chose three random words,
peas, trees... and hummingbirds."

1. What was good about the password created in the story?

2. What are random words?

3. Why does choosing three random words help to make a more secure password?

Three Random Word Passwords

Big Bubba's password was good because it was random.

If something is random it means it is hard to predict. Random means chosen by chance — words or objects that are all very different, in an unusual and unexpected combination.

By choosing three random words, Bubba's password was even harder to guess — and therefore more secure!

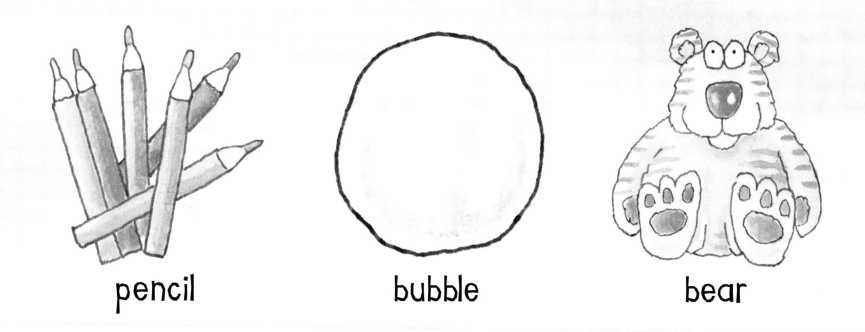

pencil   bubble   bear

Make a Password Generator

Use the dice net to make your own three random word password.

1. Carefully cut the following page out of the book along the dotted line.

2. Cut out the dice net along the outer dotted lines.

3. Write a random word in each square, and draw a picture to go with it
   e.g. lollipop, cloud, mouse.

4. Fold along the inner lines.

5. Shape into a cube/dice shape.

6. Glue the tabs inside.

Roll the dice three times in a row to create a three random word password!

If you roll the same word twice, roll again - remember it needs to be three random/different words.

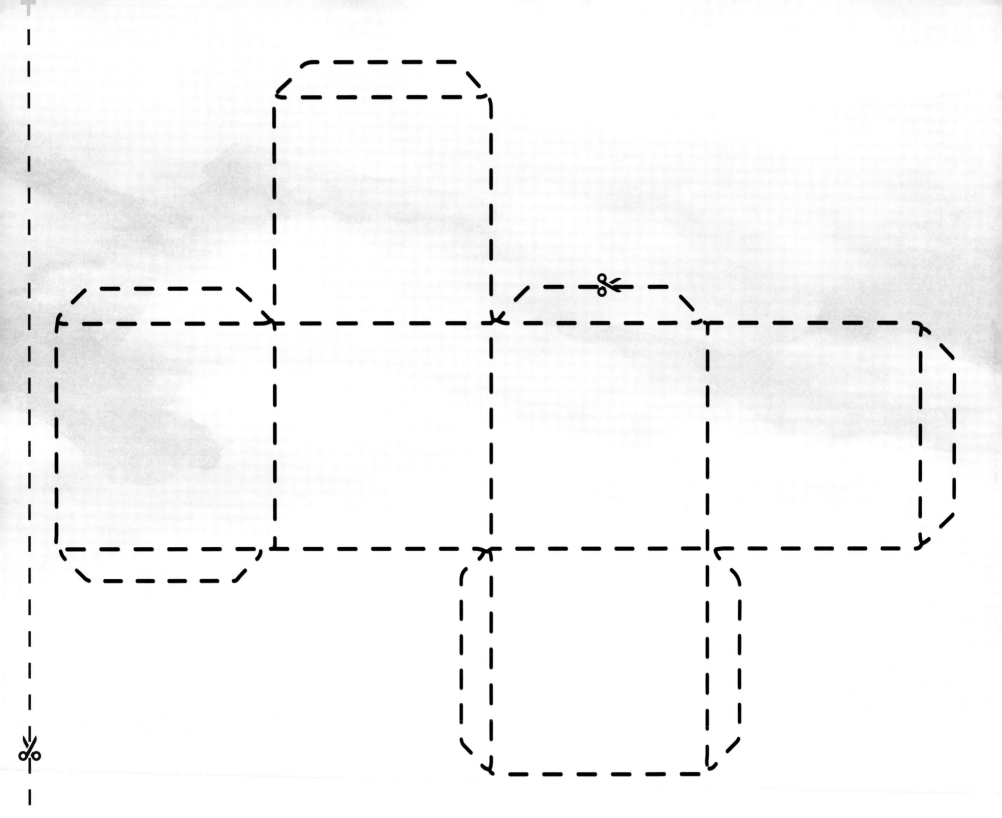

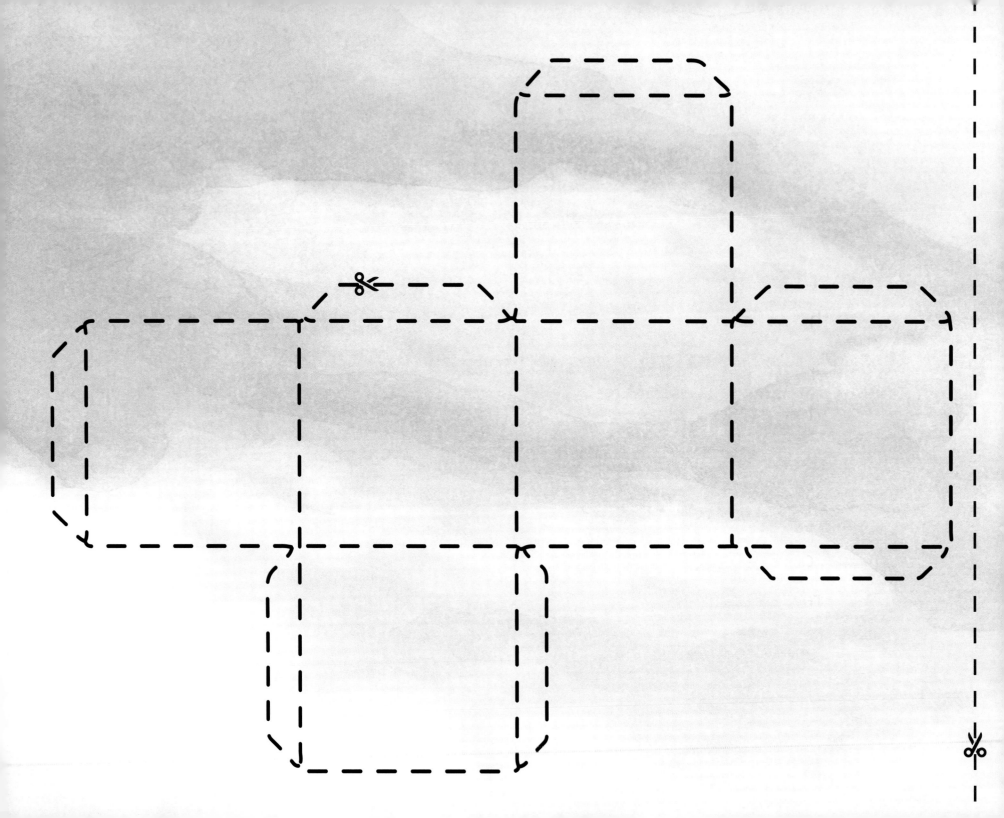

Glossary

Key cyber security vocabulary and definitions.

passcode - a series of letters, numbers, etc. that you must provide in order to access a computer or other electronic device

password - a series of letters, numbers, etc. that you must type into a computer or computer system in order to be able to use it, or a secret word or phrase that you need to know in order to be allowed into a place

protected - to make sure that somebody/something is not harmed, injured, damaged, etc.

random - done, chosen, etc. without somebody deciding in advance what is going to happen, or without any regular pattern

secure - to protect something so that it is safe and difficult to attack or damage

Definitions from Oxford Learners Dictionary correct as of June 2024

Visit theBongles.com
for fun learning activities
and animations.

Other Bongles Books

Jessie and Nessie

Pet Washing Machine

Monster Takeaway

TV Dinner